GUYKU

A Year of Haiku for Boys

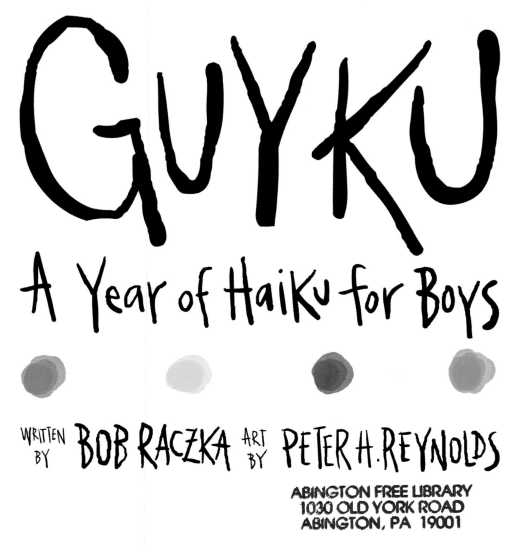

WRITTEN BY **BOB RACZKA** ART BY **PETER H. REYNOLDS**

HOUGHTON MIFFLIN BOOKS FOR CHILDREN   HOUGHTON MIFFLIN HARCOURT   BOSTON   NEW YORK   2010

Houghton Mifflin Books for Children is an imprint of
Houghton Mifflin Harcourt Publishing Company.

www.hmhbooks.com

The text of this book is handwritten.
The illustrations are watercolor and digital color.

Library of Congress Cataloging-in-Publication
Raczka, Bob.
Guyku : a year of haiku for boys / written by Bob Raczka ;
pictures by Peter Reynolds.
p. cm.
ISBN 978-0-547-24003-9
1. Haiku, American. 2. Children's poetry, American. 3. Seasons—Juvenile
poetry. 4. Boys—Juvenile poetry. I. Reynolds, Peter, 1961- ill. II. Title.
PS3618.A346G89 2010
811'.6—dc22
2009049697

Printed in China
LEO 10 9 8 7 6 5 4 3 2 1
4500221237

To my sons, Robert and Carl,
may you always appreciate
the simple things in life.
               — B.R.

To my nephews Andrew, Chris,
Simon, Mark, Josh, Nate, Ben,
James, Nick, Adam, Jason, Eric,
John, Paul, Brian, and Pat.
               — P.H.R.

The wind and I play
tug-of-war with my new kite.
The wind is winning.

I free grasshopper
from his tight, ten-fingered cage —
he tickles too much!

With baseball cards and clothespins, we make our bikes sound like motorcycles.

In a rushing stream,
we turn rocks into a dam.
Hours flow by us.

If this puddle could
talk, I think it would tell me
to splash my sister.

I watch the worms squirm
and decide to bait my hook
with hot dog instead.

Pine tree invites me
to climb him up to the sky.
How can I refuse?

Mosquito lands on my cheek. I try to slap her, but I just slap me.

Lying on the lawn,
we study the blackboard sky,
connecting the dots.

Skip, skip, skip, skip, plunk!
Five ripple rings in a row —
my best throw ever!

Penny on the rail,
you used to look like Lincoln
before you got smooshed.

With the ember end
of my long marshmallow stick,
I draw on the dark.

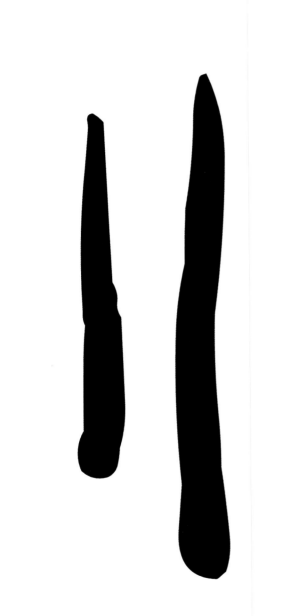

Hey, Who turned off all the crickets? I'm not ready for summer to end.

We follow deer tracks
in the mud, pretending that
we too are wild beasts.

Helicopters spin
in squadrons from our maple—
I almost caught one!

The best part about
kicking this stone home from school
is there are no rules.

From underneath the
leaf pile, my invisible
brother is giggling.

Pounding fat cattails
on a park bench near the pond,
we make a snowstorm.

Winter must be here.
Every time I open my
mouth, a cloud comes out.

How many million
flakes will it take to make a
snow day tomorrow?

Two splotches of white
on a black tree trunk. I aim
my next pitch— *strike three!*

Icicles dangle,
begging to be broken off
for a short sword fight.

It's silent under
these pine boughs sagging with snow,
like hibernating.

Last week's snowman looks
under the weather. Must be
a spring allergy.

Why I wrote Guyku

Are you a guy? Me too. I just happen to be a guy who likes haiku.

When I was a boy, I didn't even know what a haiku was. But I did spend a lot of time outside with my friends. Nature was our playground, and we made the most of it—catching bugs, climbing trees, skipping stones, throwing snowballs.

Now that I'm a grownup (sort of), I realize that haiku is a wonderful form of poetry for guys like us. Why? Because a haiku is an observation of nature, and nature is a place where guys love to be.

Haiku poems are also short. They're only three lines long, with five syllables in the first line, seven syllables in the second line, and five syllables in the third line. A haiku doesn't take long to read, but don't be fooled: a good haiku can pack a punch.

One more thing about haiku: they're written in the present tense. In other words, whatever happens in a haiku, it's happening right now. From my experience, guys are always interested in what's happening right now.

In case you were wondering, every haiku in this book is about something I did as a boy. Or something I've seen my own boys do. It's the kind of stuff I—along with amazing and inspiring illustrator Peter H. Reynolds—wanted to share with guys like you.

—BOB RACZKA

Why I illustrated Guyku...

I am SO excited about *Guyku*.

I am passionate about creativity and art—inspiring EVERY-ONE to make their mark . . . whether art, story, or poem.

My mission is also to help people defy stereotypes—to think creatively and *bravely*. The invitation for boys to swim in the "poem pond" needs to be issued more often, and more loudly.

I want to shout, *"Come on in! The water's fine!"*

Bob Raczka's haikus are wonderfully clever, universally delightful, and filled with old-fashioned boyish fun. What a thrill it is to link arms with Bob on this poetic romp—and important mission!

— PETER H. REYNOLDS